# The Little GREEN Hen

Alison Murray

ORCHARD

Once, on top of a hill,

grew a beautiful, old and

# very fruitful

apple tree.

And in the hollow of its trunk lived a little green hen.

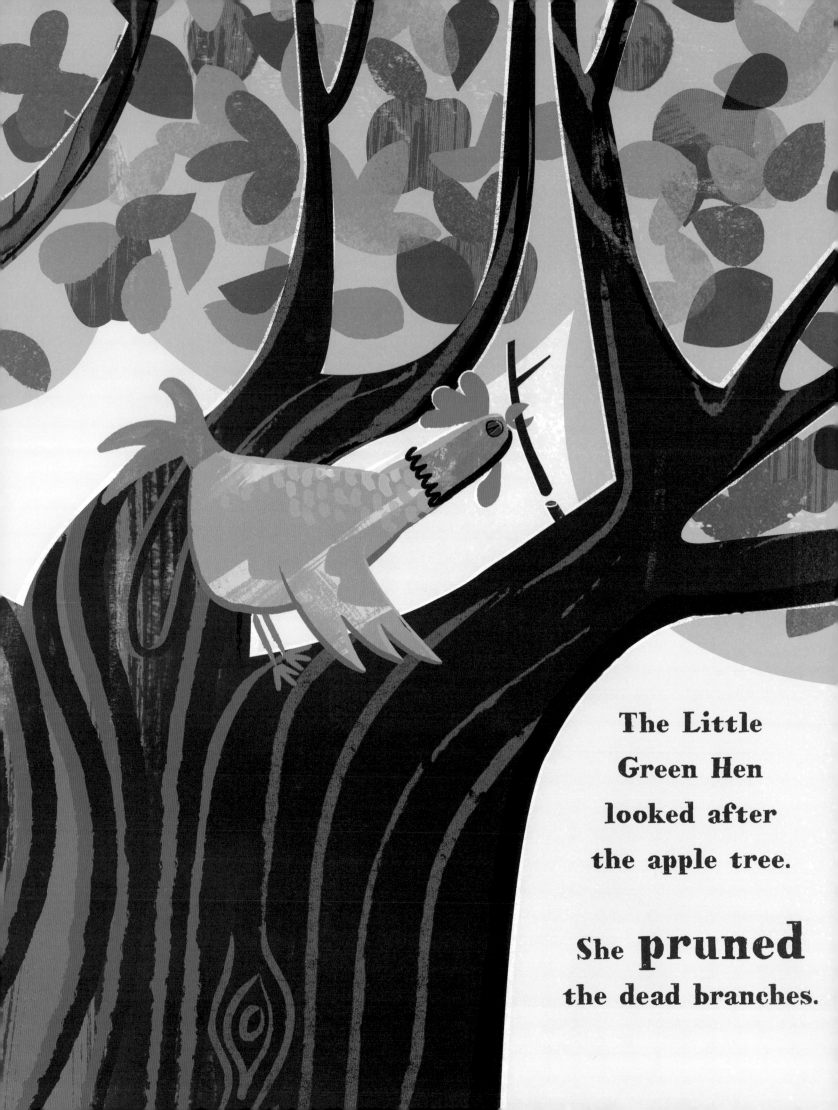

The Little
Green Hen
looked after
the apple tree.

She **pruned**
the dead branches.

She kept the **pests** under control

and she sowed the apple **seeds** so more trees and more apples would grow.

But as the weeks went by,
and the seeds that she had planted
began to grow, the Little Green Hen
realised that she needed some help
to look after her new orchard.

"Who would like to help me tend the apple trees?" asked the Little Green Hen. "The branches need pruning."

"Not I," said Peacock. He was far too busy preening himself.

"I will," said Dog,
who loved sticks.

"Who will help me keep the pesky bugs from eating all the leaves?" asked the Little Green Hen.

**"Not I,"** said Fox, who was much more interested in eating the Little Green Hen.

"I will," said the teensy brown sparrow, who was partial to pesky bugs.

"And who will help me sow the apple seeds?"
"**Not I**," said the fat ginger cat,
who was far too busy lounging
on a log in the sun.

"I will,"
said Squirrel,
who was very
good at burying
things where no
one could find them.

So the new friends helped the Little Green Hen tend the orchard – and the orchard shared its bounty with them through

# spring,

**summer** and **autumn.**

Then down came the rain.
It rained for days
and weeks and more.

The new friends stayed
warm and dry in
the old apple tree.

But Peacock couldn't stay in his hydrangea bush – the pond was overflowing.

And Fox couldn't stay in his den, which was filling up with water.

Luckily there was just enough room
for them all on Cat's log . . .

which drifted away across the flood water . . .

until . . .

"Look, it's the old apple tree," cried Cat.
"Maybe the Little Green Hen will help us!

Quickly, row!"

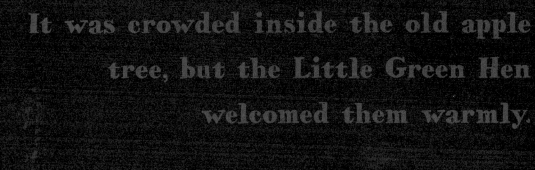

It was crowded inside the old apple
tree, but the Little Green Hen
welcomed them warmly.

**Together**
they waited
for the rain
to stop.

Eventually the sun came out and
the flood waters began to disappear.

The Little Green Hen stepped out of the
apple tree. "Who will help clean up this
mess?" she said to no one in particular.

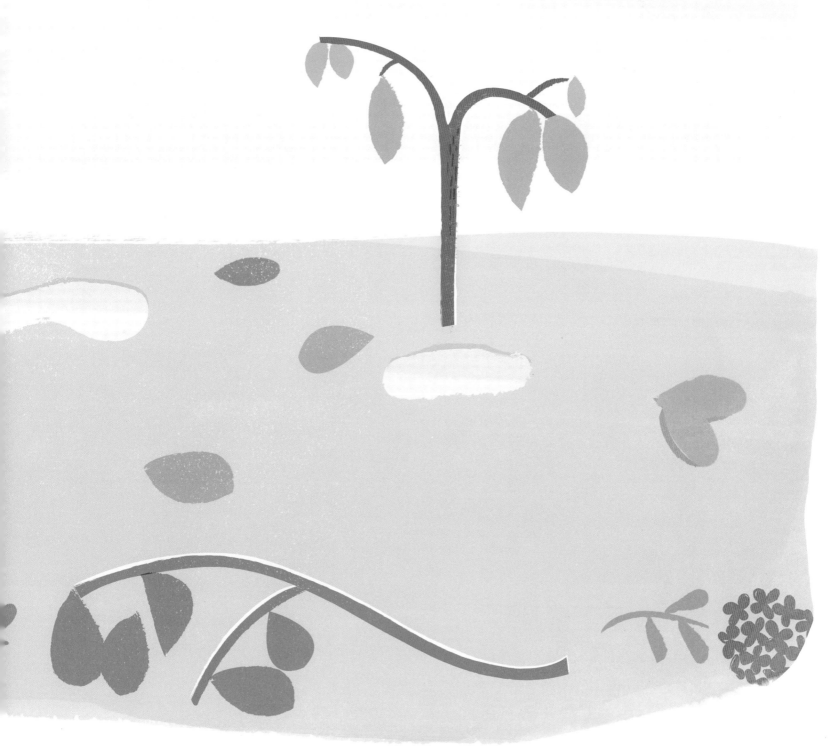

"**We will!**" said Dog,
Squirrel and Sparrow.

# "And so will WE!"

said Fox, Cat and Peacock.

The Little Green Hen
had never had so many
enthusiastic helpers.

Time passed and the seedlings grew into a beautiful orchard. The rains still came, but the thirsty young tree roots soaked up all the water and floods were rare.

The Little Green Hen and her friends looked after the orchard and the orchard looked after them. The food and shelter it provided were more than enough . . .

for everyone.